countless funny stories

ON THE SPOT

By **Amy Krouse Rosenthal and Lea Redmond**

Illustrated by **Sanne te Loo**

Random House 🏠 New York

When I woke up this morning,
what did I see?

A sweet little . . .

chirping at me.

I headed to the kitchen
to fill my rumbling tummy.

I poured a big bowl of . . .

Super-duper yummy!

Then I ran out to the garden
to water all the plants.

The . . .

had finally sprouted,
so I did a little dance!

I smelled the pretty flowers
and pulled out pesky weeds,
then planted . . .

and . . .

What unusual seeds!

I love going to the park.

The . . .

is fun to climb.

As I slide
down the . . .

I scream, "Wheeeeeee!"
every time.

I spotted my friend playing.
He was making something cool.

He shared his . . .

with me.

Such a great building tool!

Uh-oh, what was that?
It wasn't what we'd planned.

I felt a drop of . . .

land upon my hand.

I raced home on
my speedy . . .

just as fast as
I possibly could.

Luckily, I'd practiced riding it
and had gotten pretty good!

I arrived home soaking wet
and found dry clothes to wear.

Then I curled up
with my . . .

in our very
coziest chair.

Soon my father called, "Dinnertime!"
I knew it would be delicious.

Spaghetti with . . .

Also quite nutritious!

After all the dishes were washed
and bedtime stories were read,

I found my cuddly
stuffed . . .

waiting on my bed.

Twinkle, twinkle, little . . .

It's my favorite song to sing!

Then I closed my eyes and wondered
what the next day might bring.

THIS DOESN'T HAVE TO BE THE END!

Rearrange the objects or stickers you
just used, or try some new ones.

Now another funny story
awaits you!

★ ★ ★

Visit us on the Web! randomhousekids.com

Educators and librarians, for a variety of teaching tools,
visit us at RHTeachersLibrarians.com

Library of Congress Cataloging-in-Publication Data
is available upon request.

ISBN 978-1-101-93230-8 (trade) —
ISBN 978-1-101-93231-5 (ebook)

MANUFACTURED IN CHINA
10 9 8 7 6 5 4 3 2 1
First Edition

SPOTLIGHT ON THE CREATORS

The authors are Amy Krouse Rosenthal and Lea Redmond. Amy writes books for children like **Little Pea, Spoon,** and **Uni the Unicorn** and books for grown-ups like **Encyclopedia of an Ordinary Life** and **Textbook Amy Krouse Rosenthal.** Lea is the creator of **The World's Smallest Post Service** and the author of **Knit the Sky.** She designs journals such as **Letters to My Future Self** and playful objects like **Seed Money** and **Recipe Dice.**

Even though Amy lives in Chicago and Lea lives in Oakland, California, they love collaborating. This is their first book together.

Sanne te Loo is the illustrator of several award-winning picture books published in her native home, the Netherlands. Her most recent book, **The Mermaid's Shoes**—which she wrote and illustrated—is available in the United States. Sanne lives in the historical district in Utrecht, the Netherlands, with her husband, who is a painter, and their two children.